THE BIRTHDAY BEE

BY ANNA KOPP

AN UNOFFICIAL MINECRAFT BIRTHDAY STORY FOR EARLY READERS

For my boys, whose love of Minecraft
fuels their love of reading.

It's Buzzy the Bee's birthday. Buzzy is excited to have a birthday party.

But first, Buzzy must collect
pollen for the hive.
A birthday is no excuse for
slacking off.

Buzzy goes to the poppy field. There are many red flowers.

"Happy birthday, Buzzy," says Hop the Rabbit.

"Thank you," says Buzzy, "I can't wait to get home for my party."

Together, they go to the dandelion field. Buzzy buzzes between the yellow flowers.

"Happy birthday, Buzzy," says Red the Fox.

"Thank you," says Buzzy, "I can't wait for my party."

They go to the cornflower field. Buzzy zooms around the blue flowers.

"Happy birthday, Buzzy," says Woof the Wolf.

"Thank you," says Buzzy, "I'm excited for my party."

Buzzy is finally full of pollen.
It's time to go to the party!

"Can I come to the party?" asks Hiss the Spider.

"No way," says Buzzy, "you're too scary."

"I'm scared of foxes," says Hop, "but not Red."
"And I'm scared of wolves," says Red, "but not Woof."

"That's true," says Buzzy. "I'm sorry, Hiss. You can come to the party."

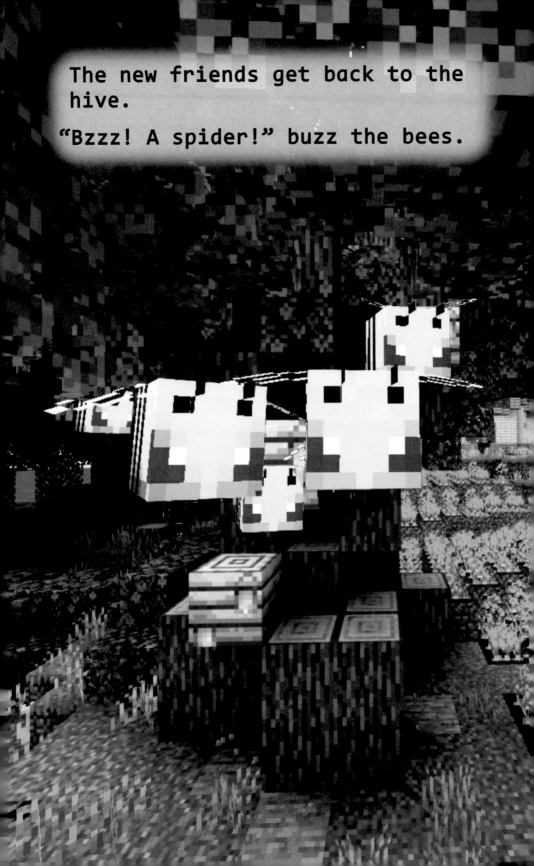

The new friends get back to the hive.

"Bzzz! A spider!" buzz the bees.

Hiss spins web decorations.